**IMAGINE THAT**

Licensed exclusively to Imagine That Publishing Ltd
Tide Mill Way, Woodbridge, Suffolk, IP12 1AP, UK
www.imaginethat.com
Copyright © 2015 Imagine That Group Ltd
All rights reserved
2 4 6 8 9 7 5 3 1
Manufactured in China

Written by Ellie Wharton
Illustrated by Amanda Enright

ISBN 978-1-78958-607-7

A catalogue record for this book is available from the British Library

# A big day for a little princess

Written by
**Ellie Wharton**

Illustrated by
**Amanda Enright**

Princess Clarissa leapt out of bed like a lamb in springtime. She had barely slept a wink ... today was the day of the royal wedding and she was going to be a bridesmaid!

She skipped happily over to her bedroom window,
but then shrieked in dismay ...

The weather was frightful! Black clouds swirled, rain lashed down and the strong wind had whipped the washing line away ... and with it her beautiful bridesmaid dress! Disaster! How would she get it back in time for the big event?

Luckily, Princess Clarissa was a clever sort of princess
and just then she had a save-the-day kind of idea.
Sir Doug the royal dog and his nifty nose
would find the dress, of that she was certain.

But where exactly was Sir Doug?

Princess Clarissa searched every nook and cranny of the castle, but the royal pooch was nowhere to be found.

Finally, she came to the pantry ...

Creeeaaaakkkk ...

went the pantry door.

'Woooooooffff!'

barked Sir Doug.

And there he was, buried head first in the five-tiered, fabulously yummy and ridiculously rich, royal wedding cake.

'Double disaster!' exclaimed Princess Clarissa, as Sir Doug looked up at her guiltily, his nose covered in sugary sprinkles.

Now the princess had not one, but two big problems. It was definitely more than one princess could possibly handle ... time to get some help of the magical kind!

'A one and a two and a magical three ...'

... dear Fairy Godmother, please help me!'
Princess Clarissa sang, twirling around
on the tips of her toes three times.

'Yes, yes, yes!'

exclaimed an elderly fairy appearing
in a cloud of sparkles before her.
'What can I do for you, my dear princess?'

Princess Clarissa explained the double disaster she had on her hands.

'Hmmm, I see ... well, I can give you three wishes,' said Fairy Godmother. 'But use them wisely, they're all I've got time for today.

The wedding season is a busy time for fairy godmothers, don't you know!'

Luckily, Princess Clarissa was very wise,
so she had already thought of three wishes.

'I wish ...

1. To find my bridesmaid dress!

2. To get another fabulously yummy and ridiculously rich royal wedding cake!

3. To get rid of this horrid weather!

Fairy Godmother waved her wand three times and ...

Pop!

Pop!

Pop!

Pop!

Before she could say 'Get me to the church on time!'
Princess Clarissa was holding a giant ten-tiered wedding cake
and dressed in her pretty pink bridesmaid dress. The birds
were singing, the sun was shining and a big rainbow arched
over the church. Hooray! She had saved the day!

The wedding was a great success and even Sir Doug redeemed
himself, carrying the rings down the aisle in a velvet pouch.

But as the happy couple left the church and people threw colourful confetti, Princess Clarissa realised she had forgotten to wish for the most important thing of all ...

'One, two, three ...

**Wheeee!'**

shouted the bride,
throwing the bouquet
over her shoulder ...

Princess Clarissa jumped up as high as she could ...
but she was only little, and she couldn't reach as high
as the other girls.

Suddenly, a gust of wind pushed her up into the air.
The little princess grabbed the bouquet, and landed
as gracefully as a ballerina.

It had been a big day for a little princess.
Princess Clarissa's grin spread from ear to ear.

The wedding was a royal success and everyone agreed that Clarissa had been the best bridesmaid ever!

Woof! Woof!